THE KISS THAT ALMOST KILLED ME

Sometimes the truth is in the joke

ANNIE JOHNSON

THE KISS THAT ALMOST KILLED ME

Copyright © 2020 by Annie Johnson

ISBN

PRINTES IN UNITED STATES OF AMERICA

This book is a work of fiction. The events and characters described herein are imaginary and are not intended to refer to specific places or living and dead persons. The opinions expressed in this manuscript are solely the opinions of the author. Any resemblance to actual persons, living or dead, or actual events is purely coincidental.

AWJ Production

http://www.awjproduction.com

To my Lord and Savior Jesus Christ
for once again letting me do your mighty work and for
the gifts you gave me. To my family; you guys really
rock. Thank you for your love and support. To my
grand- baby Harley. Grammie loves you so much, and I
can't wait to see how God is going to use you in a
mighty way.

Foreword

From the first time I read her first book
"The Cry Nobody Heard", I knew it was going to be another bestseller, inspired from her essence of grace transferred to paper. Annie Johnson has all the qualities of high-flying performances, from the stage now to paperback and hardcover books, where her every word speaks life. Today, as I write this foreword with honor, I had the opportunity to experience firsthand her motivation, encouragement, and inspiration through my own journey. Allow this book to minister to you, and find your way out of negativity to enter a world of forgiveness and hope through the words of this woman of God.

Dinah Freeman, Owner DKay Styles

Introduction

Sometimes adults never let go of the childhood pain caused by someone they loved dearly: especially a woman whose daddy walked out on her at a young age. Sometimes she remains chained to the pain of trying to figure out what love really is and how a man should love her—things fathers should always prepare their daughters for. *"The Kiss That Almost Killed Me"* will take you on a roller-coaster ride that forces you to deal with different emotions. How you choose to handle the experience is entirely up to you. Often, we put ourselves in situations and relationships without consulting God, mainly because we get impatient, envious, and too stubborn to do things the right way, and we don't get to choose the consequences. In this book, my prayer is that you will receive wisdom, forgiveness, and answers to unknown questions you may have pondered about. Please allow this book to minister to you and to encourage you to keep pushing, trust God, and know that everything has a way of working itself out in due time. *"The Kiss That Almost Killed Me"* is a work of fiction from the Annie Johnson Collection.

"Waiting on God really pays off only when you truly listen to him."

Chapter One

My Life...

On my way to a happy life, being in love is a great thing. Especially when you have someone who loves you back. And that's exactly what I have, a true love, someone who loves me back. At least that's what I thought. I can tell you this up front; if it hadn't been for the Lord on my side, there's no way I would have made it. My story starts when I was twenty three years old. I thought I had found the man of my dreams. He was everything I ever wanted, everything I asked God for. Okay, maybe I didn't completely wait to get confirmation from God. But I just knew in my heart he was the one. I often ask myself why did I stay? Why did I let this man take everything that I believed in away from me? If only I had waited on God. But, there are times we feel that God is moving too slowly, so we become impatient and start doing things on our own. But, I'm so glad God still loves me unconditionally. There is nothing I can do that would change the love God has for me. How do I know He loves me? Because I'm able to tell you my story. Here goes.

My whole life I have been this good little girl who always did everything that my mother told me to do. I was raised with family values, and I was raised to be Christian. It's funny how God does things. My mother is really my grandmother, because my mother died when I was seven years old, and my father, well let's say I haven't seen him since I was eighteen. Let me explain this to you. My dad was not married to my mother. Yep. He was cheating on his wife with my mother. I can remember back when I was ten years old, I met him for the first time. He came to my grandmother's house and introduced himself to me as my father. I guess you can say I looked a lot like him, so he couldn't deny me. All I remember is him telling my grandmother if she needed anything for me, to please let him know. And he gave her a contact number, gave me $5, and rubbed me on my head and said I will be seeing you later. One thing I can tell you is he was true to his word because I didn't see him for a very long time. He didn't stay long, and I really didn't care, because I didn't know him. But, he took care of me until I turned eighteen, and then he dropped me like a hot potato. I remember my grandmother calling him and asking if he could spare some money to help send me to college. He said I was grown and could take care of myself. My grandmother was so hurt. I knew there was no way she could send me to college. She didn't make enough to do that. And besides, it really wasn't her responsibility. But, my dad made it quite clear that he was out. He retired himself from being my father. In other words, if I was thinking about going to college, I was on my own. I couldn't believe he could do this to me. What did I do that was so wrong? Why did he hate me so much? I started rationalizing, did I take it the wrong way? Was I too young to really understand where he was coming from? I was heartbroken. So many things I wanted to tell him and so many things I needed him to teach me. I didn't know what to expect from a man or know how a man love me. It was my father's job to teach me those things. I didn't know him, I feel it was his job to try to build a relationship with me. You know what some people say. Men make babies, and women raise them. All I know is it's so important for a father to have a relationship with his daughter because it helps her define her relationship with men and life. Yes. If only he was around, I could have made better choices. If I would see him today, I would say you left me daddy. You left a big void in my life, and now I don't know what it means to be loved. I don't how a man should love me and how much of myself I should give to him. You left me hanging. And because of that, I made lots of poor choices. It was your responsibility to be my provider, protector and to encourage me to be a better me. You could have saved me daddy from myself, but I forgive you. Yes. I forgive you. When I think about that word "forgive" it is easy to say and even harder to fulfill. As I speak through my broken heart, what I want you to understand is that when my dad dismissed me, it affected me in a bad way. In my flesh, I felt that I hated all men, but in my spirit, I carried God, and He got me through it. So, I made a promise to myself. I promised that if I saw him, again I would forgive him. I would make peace with him for my soul's sake. You need to be careful about what you say. Paul said, When I try to do what is right, evil is always present. I just want to make peace, and if this is a test I am about to go through, I'm bound to pass it because I want to serve God for real. The devil will try to make a fool out of you every time. I remember one day I was on my way to church when I seen my dad at a gas station. I asked Sister Dinah to pull over so I could speak to him. I jump out with this big smile on my face, I go to hug him. But before I could touch him, he put his hand out for me to shake like I was a stranger to him. Then, this full- figured woman approached his car. She asked him who I was? And what came out his mouth next would have killed me if I was not strong in my relationship with God. He introduced me as his co-worker's, daughter. I thought that was low of him. He also introduced me to his two other children, who looked just like me, but I played it cool. I played his game. I excused myself and wished them a great day. As I walked away, tears flowed down my face. The devil tried to tell me to turn around and give him a piece of my mind, but I rebuked him in the name of Jesus because I knew who I was and who I belonged to. I'm a child of God. So, I got back in the car with Sister Dinah and we drove away. I was so hurt, but I had to motivate myself to find my strength to carry on. And then a scripture came to mind. *My strength is made perfect in my weaknesses.* Yes! I was strong. I was strong enough to walk away and never look back. I knew from that day he was not the person I ever wanted to be. That day, I learned that life sometimes can be a setback for a comeback. This was not the first time I had been hurt. But, God kept me then, and I know he will keep me now. So, I happily looked to the future because I knew God would take care of me.

Chapter Two
My Journey Begins

First day in college, feeling very uncomfortable, no familiar faces around. I'm the new kid on the block, or so I thought. My first class was full of my old high school classmates, even the ones I thought wouldn't graduate. Wow. Now this is a great start of the first day as a freshman. Seems like old times. The girls and I back together again. Even the ones I didn't care much for. But anyway, after my third class, I was tired and ready to go home. When the clock struck two, I was out. Yes, it was time to go. I rushed to my car and bumped into this good- looking guy. And he said are you okay. I said I am now. Now where did that come from? I have never been so straight- forward before, but what the heck I'm not a little girl anymore. He asks me my name. I told him, and he told me his name was Bruce. Before I could get a conversation going, his girlfriend walked up. I couldn't believe that he was dating Big Butt Betty.

When she was in high school, they called her the get-around girl. I spoke to her, and she looks at me very pompous and said, 'Hey'. I'm like heifer you could have kept that. But, I waved her off and proceed on to my destination. I knew it was too good to be true. I never had any luck with the cute guys. I guess that's because I wasn't the type who gave up the booty. Not that I didn't want to, but I was too scared to. I was scared of having to face my mother. I feel I owe her so much, and the least I could do is try to live right. This a daily fight for me. Is it hard for you? Listen, there are times in our life when we hold on to some things we really need to let go of. When you hold on and do not give yourself to God, you can't heal. If you want a breakthrough, if you want to heal, you need to fight for it. You can learn many things, but no one can teach you faith; you have to live by faith. If you have never been through anything, you won't understand what I'm talking about. But, if you have been through something, if you had to cry in the midnight hour, or laugh to keep from crying, then you understand what I'm talking about. See, God can make a way where there was none before. He can turn your mess into a message. He can turn your problems into praise. There were times I was playing church, but now I'm too busy trying to get into heaven.

Chapter Three
Home Sweet Home…

What a long day it has been for me. Church and school are wearing me out. But I won't complain because God has been too good to me. Finally, home sweet home. And my mother has it smelling good up in here. Funny, I thought she had to work today. I was hoping I would have the house to myself. But it doesn't look like that's going to happen. Maybe if I tiptoe in, she won't hear me. As I tiptoe to my room, but then I heard funny noises coming from my mother's room. I know what's going on. I couldn't believe she's getting it in. And it sounds like she's with Deacon Sunny. I knew he wasn't hanging around here for nothing. But that's okay. It's all good. I'm going to let her make it. Oh, forget it I'm going to knock on her door. Momma, are you okay? I can hear her telling him to be quiet. Are you okay mother? She says yes, in a low, soft voice. So I just open the door and catch her and Deacon Sunny in the act of getting it on. All I said to her was everything you tried to teach me just went out the window. I told her if you are going to get it on, I'm going to get it on too. Deacon Sunny has the nerves to say wait a minute girl I'm a one- woman man. I'm like are you out your mind? Do you really think I want any part of you? I was so disappointed in my mother. All she did was look at me with embarrassment and shame, and I didn't even care. She let me down. All my life, I been saving myself for marriage, but now she's up in here having sex with someone she's not married to. Another let- down. I'm learning real fast that all I have to depend on is God and myself. She can forget about me going to church with her tonight. I think it's about time I made my own plans. Yes, it's time for me to let my hair down. Lord, I'm so hurt right now. I have no control over how I feel. God, all my life I lived by every inch of your word, but I'm so tired of being let down and walked upon. I feel so betrayed. Lord, please tell me how do I get myself out this rut? Why does everybody cause me so much pain? Lord, I only feel appreciated when I can give something. I feel like nobody under-stand me. I feel like nobody cares about me. I have lost my trust in my mother, and my mind has been taken hostage.

Chapter Four
Living My Life ...

Living my life like it's golden, and I'm so happy. I'm making my paper, feeling like I can conquer the world and I so deserve it; I've worked very hard for this. I feel like I can do anything. The sky isn't the limit; I can go far beyond it. Four years have passed, and my life has been turned upside down. I guess you can say I started doing my own thing. Living a secret life can really take a toll on you, especially when you can't keep your stories straight. I'm so tired of pretending I have to find a way to tell my mother that I'm not her perfect little daughter. You see, I have been pregnant twice, and both times, I had to have an abortion because I was not married and I was a leader in the church. There was no way I could tell my mother that. I'm sure she would be slain in the spirit with grief calling and telling the Lord on me. I'm really trying to get my life in order. I can't allow my past to control my future; it is time for a change. Now that I'm a grown woman, I am choosing to wait on true love who knows what the future holds. I'm here at this conference, and baby, it's looking good up in here. Wait a minute, I can't believe who I'm seeing right now. It's Bruce Daniels my college crush. And dang, that boy still has it going on. He's one of the guest speakers and baby, I can't take my eyes off of him. From the time I enter the room, my eyes are locked on him. Okay, maybe I'm exaggerating a little, but you get the point. Now keep in mind that the room was full of handsome, good Christian men. Wow! Have I just died and gone to heaven, because it's so lovely to see all these hunks up in here. Although, it was a conference for singles. I was feeling real selfish. Baby, let me tell you, I let it be known that I was rolling solo. I tuck my clutch purse under my arms and I walk over to introduce myself to him. I knew I had his attention; I knew he liked what he saw, so I instantly changed my strut from neutral to overdrive. My hips and thighs had his eyes. Anyway, I introduce myself. He grabs my hand and says, It's good to see you again, Sadie, in his sexy baritone. I almost died, I said oh you remember my name. He said how could I forget a woman like you? My body starts to heat up, and all of a sudden, I broke into a sweat. And no it was not menopause; it was him. Bruce Daniels. The man I knew I was going to spend the rest of my life with. He was everything I prayed for. Everything I knew I wanted in my life. The night was young, so he excused himself to go and speak to someone he knew. As he walks away, I have to ask the Lord to forgive me, because I was lusting after a man I didn't really know I was way too attracted to his outer appearance and didn't have a clue what his heart was like or who it belonged to. All I knew is that man was fine. Okay, I need to get my thoughts in order. I have to quickly remind myself of a scripture: *"Don't look at his appearance or how tall he is, because I have rejected him. God does not see as we see. We look at outward appearances, but the LORD looks into the heart."* I have to keep my feelings tucked away in my heart all night long. I must say, being a Christian woman is not easy because if God was testing me, I truly failed. Oh no, guess who just walked in the door. It's Sister Mattie. I'm telling you, I wish the Lord had sent anybody but her. She is going to tell on me, sure as my name is Sadie. Here she comes. Wait a minute. She didn't even see me. No, no, no. There goes motor mouth Sister Rita. She talks about everything and everybody. And she is a man stealer. I know for sure she took a couple of women's husbands at the church and she doesn't care as long as she gets her coins. There's no shame in her game. She'll let you know up front, you got to pay to play. I really don't associate myself with her. She just a bit too much for me, but my mother always told me it cost you nothing to speak, and that's what I did. I spoke to her and would you believe she gave me the cold shoulder I'm like girl bye. I went to take my seat and watch motor mouth work the room. It is men everywhere. For a moment I thought I was in a club. Looked like everyone rehearsing a holy dance and shouting. This environment was different from what I was used to. I'm telling you I have seen a woman shout, her lace front fell off, she stops in the middle of her shouting to put her lace front back on and reposition her plucked middle part, and then she proceeded with her shout. I look at her and shaking my head. I tell you, some people like flirting with hell. Wait a minute who am I fooling? I can't talk about anyone up in here because I'm all up in my flesh. Anyway, I had to find myself a seat because it was time to pray. Of course I need to position myself so he could see me. He begun to pray, I drop my head and close my eyes, but I felt someone watching me. So I slightly peeps up, and it was him, Bruce was watching me. I was intrigued by that man. I couldn't believe this was happening to me. A little country girl like myself. I didn't know anything about dating. But I was willing to learn. I was ready to be loved, and I was surely ready to give it. For too long, I have given all my time to people who never gave me anything in return, well, I take that back they gave me a thank you and two babies. Bump that! I feel like Diana Ross. "I want muscles." So I looked at Bruce and I give him a little smirk and continued on in prayer. All of a sudden, I hear someone clear their throat several times in a very annoying way. I look up once again. It was these women giving him the eye. I'm like Lord Help me out here because I didn't come here to fight anybody, but if this woman comes up in my face it's on. See, that's what I'm talking about; the devil really doesn't play fair. He set us up every time. Here I am a Christian woman at a Christian event and all is on my mind is finding me a man. When the prayer was over, it was time for fellowship. I paraded my curvy brown self around the room because I knew I was someone you didn't want to miss. I'm sure I'm not the only one guilty of that. So, it was time for us to make our way to the dining room for our lunch. Bruce pressed his way thru the crowd to get to me, so of course I was walking in slow motion. I was not in a hurry to move to the dining room. I waited around for him. And all of a sudden motor mouth pops up trying to hold a conversation with me. I guess she couldn't find herself a victim so she comes over to me to waste my time. I'm looking at her like why? This chick don't even like me, and I'm not too thrilled about her. Which is sad because we both attend the same church. This woman never has two words for me, and now she wants to hold a whole conversation. Her mouth is moving and so are my eyes. I politely excuse myself. I saw Bruce, and I wanted to make sure he saw me. Before he reached me, there was that woman again, two women in fact, I'm like let me leave him alone, because seems like he has a lot going on and I'm not down with the drama. So of course I go on my way. But then, I heard him call my name. I stop in my tracks and turn around and wait with my polished pose. He is walking toward me, and I am feeling some kind of a way I can't explain. I have never been this attracted to any man. Not like this. I can't quite figure out what the attraction was. Maybe because he was a man of God. A man with power, or just maybe because he was so damn sexy even his sweat was refreshing and not to mention his pants were so tight; I could see his blessings below. Before he reached me, this same woman cut in front of him, saying to me, this is not a good man. I don't know why people can't see that. She went on to say walk away baby and don't look back because if you don't, you will be sorry later. By that time, Bruce had called for security to throw the woman out. Everyone around was saying things like who let her in here? The woman looked like she was on hard times and my heart went out to her. She was yelling and crying, telling people not to judge her because we don't know her story. Motor mouth walked over to her to talk to her and then the woman left. Motor mouth came to stand by me, and I asked her what all that was about. She walked away from me saying you will soon find out. I'm like what that mean? That heifer look at me and laugh and said I don't kiss and tell. I was convinced she was crazy. It's is really a trip up in here. It seems there were secrets going on up in here. People know stuff, but they were too scared to talk. I could see the muscle in some of their eyes pumping way too fast. So, when it was all over, I ask him what was going on and he said Sister Bernice, we have been having problems with that woman coming to the church and hassling members. Then of course he changed the subject, I wasn't too happy about that. I felt there was something he isn't telling me. So I tried to excuse myself, but that boy has a way with words. He knows how to have a conversation. He had my full attention, especially when he started asking me questions about myself. I feel like okay, this is good; finally a man wants to know my thoughts and dreams. A man who was willing to respect my mind and my intelligence. But for some reason I couldn't shake the fact that he changed the subject about that woman who was trying to warn me. What was their connection? I will soon find out, but for now, I'm going to roll with it. So, we talk for about an hour before we are interrupted by his mother. An unfriendly woman, and she is a Pastor. I don't think she was fit to wear the robe. She wore a tight black dress, with her red bottom shoes, and hot pink shiny lipstick and she told Bruce to wrap up our conversation because it was time for the next section. I could tell she rules over him, I thought to myself in order for him to be with me, he had to divorce his mother first. I'm not down with a mama's boy. Although he was very intriguing to me, and he had goals and dreams, his mother wouldn't let him go. I know all I need is time, time for him to get to know me and I Him. I was willing to see what the end was going to be, as long as I was in his future. So I said to him well you better get back before your mother comes back. He said to me, I'm not worried about her. He said I want to make sure you sit somewhere I can see you. I am like okay. With a big Kool-Aid smile. He walked me to the front row holding my hand. All those other women looked at little ole me getting escorted by the best-looking man in the house. And I was loving it. I didn't know I was setting myself up for failure because I wanted him too bad. I knew he would become my God because at the beginning, all I seen was him. From the time my eyes met his, it was like God who? There are times we treat the church like a club, we go for the wrong reasons. I guess we so busy playing church we never get to experience God.

Chapter Five

My First Date With Bruce ...

I am so excited about my first date with Bruce. I really want to look my best tonight because I want him to have eyes only for me. But after looking in my closet, and realizing I won't be able to keep his attention, you better believe I rushed out to the newest fashion boutique. I settle at DKay's fashion, trying on everything trying to look my best. I came across this sweet little black dress cut lower in the front than I normally wear, but what the heck? It's the twenty- first century, and I'm going to do this. I gaze at myself in the mirror truly liking what I seen, I told the sales person this it, I will take it. That's until she told me the price 450.00 Dollars? I said well okay, but in the back of my mind, I said he better be worth it. After finishing up at the boutique I rush home to prepare for my date. When I pull up to the driveway, I shout out, oh no, not the sisters from the church. That's all I need is for them to tell me what I should and should not be doing with my life. It's not like they have a man, and it don't look like they will ever get one. I made my way to the door, I pause for a minute, then I ran in the house quickly to my room and of course my mother asked me to reenter the room to speak to her guests. I spoke and endure how they look at me with their nose turned to the air like they were better than me. I didn't understand why my mother deals with them. But anyway, I was not going to let them stop my vibe; all that was on my mind was Bruce. I excused myself and went to get myself ready for my date. As I exit the room, I can hear one of the sisters say to my mother, Sadie hips sure are spreading. I heard my mother reply to her I'm sure you can relate to that. I said well you go momma. I ran upstairs, took my shower, did my makeup, and put on the bad sexy dress I bought just for him. I stood in front of the mirror coaching myself. Saying Sadie remember you are a Christian woman, keep your knees close together. I had to laugh at myself, but then the doorbell rings. I knew this was it, this was the moment I been waiting for, for 23 years-for a man to come and scoop me up on a date. For the first time, I didn't have to sneak around. I could hear mother and the sisters from the church talking to him. I was very impressed how he was able to carry the conversation. So I finished up and went downstairs to relieve them of their duties. My mother looks at me along with the sisters from the church, and they were speechless. Mother asks me, Sadie, can I have a word with you please? I excuse myself, following behind my mother like the little girl she thinks I am just to hear her tell me that my dress was inappropriate. She had the nerves to tell me my dress was screaming "Give it to me baby." I said to her oh, just like you were giving it to Deacon Sunny. Of course she slaps me and I said to her thank you. She asks me what has gotten into you. I told her nothing yet. When I said that all she did was look at me. I politely excused myself, then Bruce and I left. About thirty minutes later we arrived at the restaurant. I was happy to be on my first date with a good- looking man. It felt great to have everyone looking at me. He's such a gentleman but, he was so different away from the church. He was really laidback, maybe a little too laidback. Some of the things came out his mouth was somewhat of a turnoff. Especially when he starts using foul language, I had to tell him I didn't approve of that language. He apologized and called me a good girl. I felt like he insulted me on the cool. Finally thing begun to mellow out. We had a couple glasses of wine and we talked about goals and dreams. I could tell this brother had a plan. He kept telling me he was going to make me his woman I was like okay. Of course I was saying it to myself. So the waitress came to ask us if we was ready to order. He said yes and ordered for the both of us I was like okay. At least the brother could have asked me what I would like to have. But I rolled with it. I thought, hey, maybe he's trying to show me the finer things in life as he has often said to me. The night was still young when we finished dinner, which was very good. By that time I start to ask him questions about his past relationship and he told me about his baby mother, but she cheated on him. He had a whole lot to say about so many things I'm not sure half of what he was saying. My phone went off. He asked me who was it. And I told him. I really didn't know why he asked me that. I start to tell him it's none of your damn business but then I kept quiet. So he turned the tables on me and asked me about my past relationships. I told him I dated a few guy's nothing Serious. He goes I know. Because you a good girl. I didn't like that phrase because I felt he was trying to be rude and he could see I didn't approve of that, so he quickly apologized again. I said to myself okay say one more thing I'm out of here. But he calm down and begin to get very serious. He told me what he was feeling for me and how he wanted to be with me. He tried to get me to go back to his place with him, but I couldn't. I wasn't raised that way. I know if I went back to his place it was going to be all over for me. So, I told him I didn't think it was a good idea and so he took me home. We talked for a little bit and he said well I will see you around. I'm like what he means he will see me around. Then he smiled at me, and said I'm just playing. I got out the car slammed the door, and said I'm not. I thought that was very rude of him to treat me like that. He jumped out the car trying to stop me before I reached the door of my house. He begged me to stop and I did. He told me he was used to getting what he wanted. I told him you get nothing here. I mean I went off on him. But he had his way of shutting me up. He laid a kiss on me and truly I forgot about everything that happened that night. Those lips were sweeter than the red wine we have drunk. I never experienced a kiss like that, baby, it was lethal and I loved it. I had to stop him because I was two seconds from changing my no to a yes. Yeah. That kiss. What can I say about the kiss that almost killed me? Well, I think that was the biggest mistake I ever made in my life. I was wrapped up in him and he wrapped up in me. Boy, did he have me fooled.

As long as I live, I will trust God every day. What the devil meant for bad, God meant for good. If God can't change things in your life, then they can't be changed

Chapter Six

Anxiety

All day long, I have been walking around the house singing and giving thanks to God. My mother knew something was up. All she did the whole day was look at me. I tried to strike up a conversation, but she was really dry with me. I said okay mother no, I'm not pregnant. So you can relax. She looks at me and said who's worrying, that's between you and God little girl. I said mother for the last time I'm a full-grown woman and I wish you'd treat me as such. She looks me straight in my eyes and says that boy is not the one for you. He and his mother is hiding something, and I don't care if she is a minister, she's not better than the female dog I feed every day. I had to remind her that she's not perfect either. I couldn't believe my mother was talking like that. She was so full of anger. In her mind, I believe she thought they turned me against her. And it was nothing like that at all. My mother just couldn't accept the fact that I'm a grown woman who's living in her mother's house. I believe she never forgave herself for the arch she had in her back with Deacon Sunny. But she won't have to worry about feeling guilty any longer, believe me because things are about to change real quickly. As soon as Bruce gets here, all hell may or may not break loose but, either way, I'm leaving. I'm tired of everyone trying to tell me what is best for me. I know what best for me and his name is Bruce. Yes, I will be a minister's wife. I can see myself sitting on the second row with the rest of the minster's wives looking all sanctified with my big hat tipped to one side and making sure I show my high arched eyebrows. With my first lady wave cheering my man on. Daring any woman to cross the line. Yes, it's about to be a change in my life. The doorbell starts ringing. Oh, he's here. My mother sits there with her legs crossed reading her Bible. I ask if she can fix herself up a little, but she just looks at me. So I went to get the door. Bruce enters, looking and smelling so good that all I can do is think about what he's going to feel like when... well, you know I want to try to tell this story as holy as I can so please excuse me. But, anyway, Bruce arrived to ask my mother for my hand in marriage and of course she said no. She told him all the reasons she disagreed. He just sat there and let her get it all out. I mean he didn't say a word, it was like he was studying her, and he was hanging on to every word she said. So I just intervened because he was looking like he was about to change his mind, especially when she started praying. When I cut her off, she looked at me and said if you take this man as your husband, you will truly die. She said God showed her that I was in a casket. She looked at me and knew she couldn't change my mind she was fighting a losing battle because baby, I was out of there. Nothing or nobody was going to stop me from being Mrs. Bruce Daniels. I loved him, and he loved me. I knew he loved me because he never forced me to have sex with him, and he respected the fact that this time, I wanted to wait until marriage. So, I left with him that night and came home the next morning as a married woman. I got my things together and left my mother's house. Yes, I eloped because I was not willing to go through the drama of everybody trying to talk me out of marrying Bruce. I left my old life behind me. I left my church and my old friends. I joined Bruce's church. I was living the good life; at least that's what I thought. I was living a good lie. Bruce was not the man I thought he was. So many things unfolded about him, so many lies. His mother was the worst woman I ever met. It's funny. I ran a background and credit check on Bruce. The brother had everything in order. But there was one problem: his character. He was a very sick man. He almost killed me, but, God. Hallelujah!

Chapter Seven

Five Months Deep…

The ministry at the church continued to grow. Everybody who was somebody, said they were a member of the new faith church. The women came in dressed like they were going to a strip club, and the men dressed like their pimps. I felt so uncomfortable, but I learned to adapt. After church service, Bruce had preached two sermons; it seems like he was making a petition to God. It was like he was wrestling with God. He had become a very unloving man. I found myself tiptoeing around his feeling because anything could set him off. I mean anything. He had started accusing me of cheating on him when I know the only one cheating was him. I watched how the women passed him their phone numbers, gave him gifts, and had private meetings behind closed doors. The funny thing about it is that all the women were middle-aged established women with lots of money. Bruce was a young man able to give them what they weren't getting at home; Bruce was their boy toy, of course he denied it. Anytime they called for him, he was there, and he dared me to say anything about it. As time passed by, I was no longer that young naïve little girl. My eyes were wide open. I paid close attention to everything. I know when he wanted to leave the house. He would pick fights with me, or when he had been to the strip club, He said I wasn't sexy enough. I didn't change who I was. I was not going to let him turn me into one of his tricks. I didn't want to invite the enemy into my home, even though I was staring at him. I wanted so badly to throw up in Sir Bruce's face about the condom I found in his jacket pocket, but I decided to save it for another day, because I was fighting a losing battle and I was exhausted. It was time for me to get out of this marriage; I just had to figure out a way. I was so broke, I went to work every day, and he took my money and gave me a weekly allowance of $25.00. There came a time I would walk in the door and he would look at me like I made him sick to his stomach. I wanted out. I needed a way out, and it showed up on my doorstep. It was Bruce's friend Craig. Lawd that man, that man. He came over to see Bruce but of course he wasn't home. For some strange reason, I think Craig knew that. But I didn't care. I just wanted to pump him for all the information I could because the time had come for me to divorce Bruce. I offered Craig something to drink, and he sat and waited for Bruce to come home for an hour. I told Craig maybe he could try calling him. But he told me that he would just come back, so I walked him to the door and he turned to me. He said Sadie you are a good woman you don't deserve this and Bruce is not the man for you. I thought to myself, finally someone else knows I deserve better, finally I got a friend I can talk to. I began to cry, he hugged me...and then he kissed me and the bitch in me woke up. I unzipped his pants, and walked over to my purse to get the condom I found in Bruce's jacket pocket, and we made love. Was I wrong in the way I was feeling? No... Was I wrong for giving myself to him? Yes. Just for that moment I felt wanted, but as soon as it was over I felt bad. Craig tried to comfort me.

But I was too ashamed of what I done, and then he burst out laughing and said to me you really are green. Girl don't you know anything. I quickly kicked him out and ran up to my room to pack my things because I was leaving I was tired of being made a fool of, I was tired of people dumping on me, I was tired of being so lost. When I finally finish packing, I could hear Bruce coming. I told him I was leaving. He didn't take me seriously. He told me stop playing, you not going anywhere. I told him I was really leaving. He made me so angry because he kept laughing at me, then I told him since you want to laugh and make fun of me, well laugh at this: I just made love to your best friend. He looked at me and sat on the sofa. Finally I had the upper hand. He had to listen to me. I was in charge. He calmly let me go on with the details because I wanted him to hurt just like he hurt me. I mean I gave it to him. And then all of a sudden, he said I know you slept with Craig because I gave him permission to have you. My heart dropped. I said you what? He said I told Craig he could have you. You see, we had a deal and you was included in it.

He kissed me on the forehead and said, you served me well, and I thank you. I had been played. Craig had made a big fool out of me, and my husband was in on it. I thought Craig had left but he didn't. My husband walked to the door to let him in. You wouldn't believe what happened next. My husband kissed Craig. Craig was my husband's lover. I thought to myself how I could have missed this. How could I be attracted to a man who slept with other men? I didn't see it coming. I looked at him and said if you were trying to kill me well you've succeeded. I was dead inside. All I could hear my husband say was well since we are family, Craig will be going in and out from time to time. Before I knew it, I start fighting him. Throwing everything at him I could get my hands on and he punched me in the face, knocking me unconscious. The next morning I woke up in the hospital. All I remember is I tore the house up. I called for help and Bruce and the doctor walked through the door. Would you believe that fool had me admitted? He said I was on some bad drugs and yes, they found some in my system because Bruce pumped me with them. I was never the same from that day on... I was in for the fight of my life... Bruce had me just where he wanted but little did he know I was not there to stay.

I think women bring a tremendous strength and power to the table in relationships-just to be torn down when they give their heart to the wrong man

The New Me...

Well, I didn't leave him. I became hooked on the drugs. I started taking pills to go to sleep and wake up. But my white powder was my best friend. I didn't feel anything. I was in the game, and I was in it to win. He won. I finally changed the way I dressed. I became the hoe he wanted me to be. I was well put together, I was the super woman who kept a good house and took care of my husband and his man. And some of his women. We're family. That's what I told myself, and I finally began to believe it. Yep, evil wears clothes, very fine suits. I started shopping for my husband's and Craig's suits. Craig set the rules, and I abided by them. I was empty and lost. But I didn't care. My mother tried to come and take me away from here, but I couldn't share my demons with her. I had to fight for my own life. So, I turned to my mother and told her not to come to my house again. My mother was not the type of woman who would just walk away, so I had to hurt her bad enough that she would stay away. So I threw her past in her face. I asked her how she could tell me anything when she allowed her first husband to have women on the side; in fact she was friends with one of them. My mother backed out my door and told me satan has his hands on you, but he won't kill you because I asked God to spare your life. I went off on her. I mean the more I cussed her the more she blessed me. She rebuked that spirit in the name of Jesus. I didn't see my mother for months. I was in this thing. I was ready to die. Or so I thought.

Chapter Nine

Trying to Get the Monkey Off My Back…

The drugs had taken over my life. I know if I didn't get help, I was going to die. So, I joined Thelma's rehab group. My first day I stood up and said hello, my name is Sadie. I'm 25, and I am addicted to pills and cocaine and have been ever since I married satan. I tried to kick it a few times.

And this is my first time seeking professional help. I'm here because now I'm finding myself using more than I can afford, and each time I use, I lose a part of who I am. Its hell being a drug head because if you don't use anything, nothing really makes sense. I'm ready to move on with my life, put drugs behind me for good, and never look back. Man that felt good. For me to say that. The truth of the matter is I don't know if I can. It's hard to let go of something that makes you feel good. My values are completely out of whack; my priorities are skewed. Because drugs have become the primary focus of my life. My pills are my coping tool, and my powder is my master. I couldn't take it anymore, so I grabbed my purse and proceeded to the door and the counselor jumped up and said, Sadie. I stopped, and she told me if you are going to win, you have to fight this disease. Try to put as much passion, time, and energy into recovery as you put into your using. She said to leave a bad situation physically, you must first move it mentally. I waved bye to her, but in my mind, I knew she was right. I rushed out with tears in my eyes, feeling like I was having a breakthrough, but I couldn't allow myself to have it, not yet. I thought I didn't deserve it.

Chapter Ten

The Drama Continues...

So four days have passed, and I've been clean, but it was hard to fight, maybe because I was trying to do it on my own. The fifth day, my withdrawal symptoms started. I was sitting in the living room, trying to read my bible, and trying to stay focused. I was talking to myself and saying I could do it. But the dope kept calling me. So I slipped up, and I started using again I had tried countless times to quit. I tried going "cold turkey" many times, but nothing could keep me from drugs. Bruce made fun of me, my husband. He told me, girl, I classified you as a hopeless case, and he walked over to me, kicked me in my rectum, and told me to clean the house. I knew that I would either die as a drug addict or at Bruce's hands. I had no one to turn to. All of my so-called friends were done with me. So I stumbled to the kitchen, so I could take out the trash, and out of nowhere, the mailman showed up, and he said God can help you and Jesus is willing and able to set you free from any kind of evil power. I told him shut up you don't know me. He said oh, I do, and you know me too. I went to swing at him, but I fell to the ground. Before I could get up, he was gone. I thought maybe I was losing my mind or I was just visited by an angel. The funny thing about it is I believed what he said, that Jesus would take away all my pain, but fear overtook me.

That's what I called the church or I should say the building I attended. Early Sunday morning, we were in the building hearing Bruce preaching his heart out. The church was on fire. So were the women. Bruce loved the flattering looks they gave him, but I didn't care. He could sleep with the whole world. All I knew was I wasn't going to lay with his nasty self. Folks around the church knew something was going on. They talked in a way that made sure you knew they were talking about you.

I knew he was unfaithful; hell, I lived with this man. It didn't matter. Again, all I knew was he wasn't touching me. He had already broken me down. His mother had the nerve to tell me I needed to woman up and stand by my man. She told me to fix my face because I shouldn't give the other women things to talk about. I didn't understand where she was coming from. She said look here, you little green girl. Does it matter if he cheats as long as he takes care of you? I told her I didn't marry him to share him. She looked at me and said I tried to tell you and the other floozies to go on because Bruce was not what you wanted. He was good for preaching, getting the crowd stirred up. Keep the women falling out their chairs and he keep my checks coming. I ask her how she can say something like that about her son. She whispers in my ear he's not my biological son. When his daddy died, I raised him because he had nowhere else to go, and he was the next to take his father's place. Bruce's mother was a crackhead, and she came from a broken home. So you see, little green girl, you will not mess up my money. I looked at her and said in the house of the Lord, you say this? She told me with a straight face the Lord didn't build this house, I did. Then she said to me, oh by the way, tell Bruce to be at my house around 9 pm. I need him to tighten mama up. I looked at her, I and asked what did she mean? She said Bruce had been my little man since he was 18. And I don't mind sharing him. She waved her silk handkerchief in my face and said, clean yourself up. That was it, and I knew it was time for me to leave. I had to get out of this family. I knew it wasn't going to be easy, but I had to go. I walked out of the church, went and got in my car, and begged for God to forgive me. I said Lord, I hear you. I can't do this anymore. I didn't pray and wait until you sent me a man. God, I was lonely. I needed someone to love me. I thought he did. He fooled me, Lord. I have been sleeping with the enemy. Lord, if you give me the strength I need to leave, I promise to give myself to you. And any man from here on, come my way will have to go through you to get to me. Please forgive me, Lord. Create in me a pure heart, renew a steadfast spirit within me. I'm sorry Lord. I found myself being married to satan and his army. I didn't know how I was going to leave him, but all I know is I couldn't stay. I prayed until I was out of tears. I found myself whining. That's all the strength I had left. There are times in your life all you are going to have strength for is a whining. I felt myself dying, and I could hear the sister from my church, my home church, saying Little Sadie, a

Christian is never in a hopeless situation, your problem is you, you want to wait on God to do something when God is waiting on you to do something. Girl if you want to change your hopeless situation, you have to change your focus, to the extreme until you can't see nobody but God. I could see God, but I didn't trust Him.

Chapter Twelve
The Truth Stared Me In the Face…

I was minding my own business as I shopped for dinner. You know, doing the wifey thing. And you would never believe who I seen: the woman who they threw out the conference. You know the lady who tried to warn me. Sister .Bernice. I walked over to her and introduced myself. I told her where I knew her from, and she remembered. She said I know everything about you. I'm Bruce's biological mother. She pulled me by the hand, took me to the side, and filled me in, she said she knew Bruce's dad for many years because she was in a relationship with him. In other words, Bruce dad was cheating. She said I let myself get into a position of intimacy with another woman's husband. She said it started off as he was her counselor. She said their conversations were innocent; they talked about family, friends, and ministry. But one baby step led to another and then another, and before I could turn and run, I had fallen in love with him and had a baby, Bruce. She said he told her that he was going to leave his wife, but he never did, so after Bruce was born, I turned to drugs. Bruce's dad and his first wife took and raised Bruce. When Bruce turned 17, the woman he knew as his mother died. So I came back to the church just to find out that Bruce dad had remarried six months after his first wife's death. That evil woman knew about me, and how I felt. She knew I was bitter about Bruce's dad because of what he took from me. She said his wife wanted her to help her put a hit out on him. She kept saying how evil that woman. But I already knew that from the first time I met her. She had thrown this poor woman out of the church. She said the next thing she knew Bruce's dad had died from a heart problem. She contacted Bruce and told him who she was, and he laughed in her face and called her a crazy woman. I could tell she was still dealing with the pain. But, she went on to say that she promised God that she would help others avoid going through what she did because of her wrongdoing. She said she was working on getting the church shut down because of all the bad dealings going on there. She claimed she had tons of information that would send all of them to jail for a long time. She said she had a list of fraud and drug dealing cases, and that was only the beginning. I asked her why she was telling me all that and she said because she knows I want out. She told me when you are ready, let me know. But she made it clear it was going to happen with or without me. And she walked off. After talking to her, I grew angrier and more demanding. I knew that day I had to find my strength because it was time for me to take my life back.

Chapter Thirteen

The Church Meeting...

Early Saturday morning, I called some of my prayer warriors over from my old church to come and pray with me. I felt like I was losing my mind. So they asked me to tell them everything...I began to cry. I told them how evil he and his family were. And one of the sisters said "baby, let me tell you something: you can't please a fool. That demon he's dealing with has nothing to do with you. I'm almost sure those issues where there when you married him. I know what you are going through. It's going to be alright. What you need to do right now is go somewhere, where's it safe. Now you are welcome to live with me and, we will help you. I know she was serious about what she was saying, but I was too afraid to leave because of what people would say. I was tired. I wanted out, but I couldn't leave, at least not right away, but it was good to know that I had somewhere to go. Of course, I could go home. But, I was not ready to face my mother. I was not ready to hear I told you so. I didn't need that in my life right now. I was afraid of what people would say. I asked the sister how to handle that kind of gossip. God knows I was tired. Sister Mattie said girl, you can't worry about that, you have to realize some Christian that's been saved too long starts judging folk; remember only God will determine what your self-worth is because He looks at the heart. Just think about what God has already done for you. For the first time, I hoped. I had the strength to get out, although it was not going to be easy. The sisters began to pray for me. Bruce and Craig had driven up and walked into the house and ordered everyone out. Sister Mattie told him she was not going anywhere, and she pulled out her Bible and said I'm going to pray the hell out of you, satan. Bruce laughed. He thought it was a joke. I hadn't told the sisters about Bruce and his lifestyle. It's just something that was better kept to myself. Craig went to open the door and shove them out. They plead for me to come with them. I told them I would be alright, and I was. I was just fine. Because one thing I didn't have to worry about was sleeping with him. He didn't want me anymore. I was all used up, he said. The truth of the matter is that his appetite had changed; I was not what he wanted anymore. And that was fine with me. I looked at both of them and told them to let me get dinner started. I was feeling good. I had a little power and a good word. I was good for a while, and nothing they could do or say could bring me down. So as I was preparing dinner, the doorbell rang. I thought it was Sister Mattie returning, shockingly to see it was Bruce's mother, or should I say his other lover. She asked Bruce why Craig was looking so comfortable, and Bruce quickly said he was visiting. Then I figured it out. She didn't know that Bruce was Bisexual. He was nervous and didn't want her to find out. I told her to stay for dinner because we were family. So, I excused myself to go finish my dinner, and oh yes, I was about to have a good time. As the night went on the conversation at the table became more sensational. It was a pleasure to see them sweat. Since his mother had a taste for young men, I made sure to introduce her to Craig. I wish you could have seen the look on his face. So, when dinner was over, the she-devil, hung around to help me clean up. She asked me questions about Craig. She sensed something was wrong. So yes, I told her they were lovers. What did I have to lose; they didn't like me. They just kept me around because I knew too much. I knew all their dirty little secrets. How they embezzled money, cheated on their taxes, the list goes on and on. She stormed out of the kitchen and told Craig to go get his things and get out the house. Bruce was so upset with me that he rushed over to hit me, but I pulled a knife on him. I was ready, I was high off myself, and could taste victory. Craig went off on the she-devil, and she pulled out a gun and told him either to walk out the door or be sent out in a body bag. Craig left, and then Bruce ordered me to leave. The she-devil told him the hoe stays because they had too much to lose. She left right after Craig, but before she did, she told Bruce that he better stick with women. I started laughing to myself; a pimp was getting pimped. As soon as she left, I asked Bruce for a divorce, and he grabbed me around my neck and told me if I ever left him, he would kill me. The look in his eyes made me believe him. He looked so evil. It was like satan himself. I started singing Glory to God in his face, and he looked and me and called me crazy. He grabbed his coat and left. I continue to sing as loud as I could because I knew the only way I was going to survive was to pray and praise my way through.

Chapter Fourteen

Three O'Clock In the Morning ...

At 3:00 am, I got a call from Bruce's mother telling me I needed to go to the club and get him. I asked why he didn't call me if he needed my help. Of course, she played the husband card on me, and in return, I played the lover card. I told her we're family. She hung up the phone. So I put on some clothes and went down to club Getgit: nothing but whores, pimps, and players. I felt so uncomfortable and scared at the same time. Then I saw Bruce in a booth with some dude doing what he did. I told him to get up. He thought it was a joke because he started attracting the attention of whoever was around him and introduced me as his wife. I was so upset with him. I grabbed him and said, let's go. He started cursing me out, calling me every foul name he could think of, but it was cool because I was thinking wait until we get home. Before we could reach the door, Craig walked in. I guess Bruce called him and he had the nerves to say to me, I'm leaving with Craig. I politely took his hand off my shoulder, and he fell to the floor. I said, Craig get your gal and walked out the door. I could hear Craig telling Bruce he needed to handle me. I felt ready for anything and anybody, but I

was also so tired. I just wanted out. I thought about what Craig said to Bruce I quickly grab the keys to his car and left. For a brief moment I thought about driving myself off a cliff because anything was better than the way I was living. I had completely gone against my morals. I just kept driving. I didn't know what I was going to do. I even thought about going home to my mother, but I couldn't bring myself to do it. So I went home. My mind was made up. I said to myself either I'm going die or he is because I am not taking any more beatings he has already hit me one too many times, and because of him, my back has a dislocated disc. I have to take painkillers every day which I have become totally depended on. And I'm not even thirty. I don't deserve this. What did I do that was so wrong that I am being punished like this? As I sat there screaming this to God, I began to feel guilty. Guilty because I didn't pray for that man. Who was I? The sinner! The lost child! Who was I to think I deserved anything better? The issues I was facing were about to kill me. I thought oh God, I'm so rundown I can't even pray for myself. I just need someone to pray with me, I am just asking you Lord to give me the strength that I need to survive. As I was sitting on the floor, crying my heart out to the Lord, I could hear them coming up in the driveway. I reached for my cocaine because I knew if I was high, I could handle anything he dished out. But before I could get it to my nose, the voice of God told me no. Instead of me crying playing victim, I listened. I didn't move for some reason. I wasn't scared anymore. I sat there. The key turned in the door, and Bruce walked in, looking at me all crazy. I guess Craig dropped him off because he didn't come in. Bruce started picking on me. Once again with the foul language. I just looked at him. I was so scared he would force me to have sex, so I urinated on myself. When he saw that I had peed on myself, he laughed at me and called me a nasty stray dog. I looked at him and said, I want you to know you don't own me. You have no right to do this to me. I have sat and suffered in silence long enough, and I'm done. You are a corrupt man. You go to church every Sunday and preach as your life depends on it, and you come home and lay with your man, and you beat me. It's hell living a lie. Hmm? What would the congregation think of you if they knew how evil you are? See Bruce you have used the Bible to justify how you treat me, and you twist God words around; you will pay for that. I don't know what was wrong with me that out of all the men who were there the day, I laid my eyes on you. I picked a fool. Here's how it's going to go Bruce: if you ever put your hands on me again, two things are going to happen. Either you are going take the long sleep or I'm going to send you to jail.

Now take your pick. He jumped up from the sofa, and he walked over to me. I knew he was going to hit me. In fact, I stood up and gave him an invitation to do so, but he just said Goodnight and left. When he turned the corner, I fell before God on my face and said THANK YOU! Although I was still in a bad situation, I was free in spirit.

Chapter Fifteen

You Reap What You Sow...

Things had been going pretty well since the night I stood up to Bruce. I hadn't seen Craig around in months. Bruce was treating me decent. Nothing to brag about. He was staying home and even helping me clean up around the house. My mind was still made up that we were over. There was a knock at the door, and of course, it was his mother/lover. Lord, she had the nerve to make a key to my house. Nothing seemed to surprise me anymore. She looked troubled about something. She asked me to excuse myself. I did so, but I doubled back to eavesdrop. I was tired of being in the dark. Sometimes it doesn't pay to ear hustle. I heard the full conversation. She told Bruce he needed to go to the doctor because she was tested and had HIV. Bruce wasn't surprised and he didn't even react, so she started cussing and hitting him. I didn't move. Bruce was crying, and he told her she deserved everything that had happened to her. After he calm down, she changed to the subject to how she was going to scam the church. She told him people had been asking question about the finances of the church. I knew that this day would come Sister Bernice said with or without me, it was going to happen. Bruce told her to get out. She got angry again, and he shoved her out the door while she clawed at his face. I come out of the kitchen and looked at him. I asked him if I needed to go get checked. He told me yes. He grabbed his jacket and said I will see you at church; put on something nice. He left. I sat down on the sofa in shock, praying to God, let His will be done. I know God loves me. I know nothing catches God by surprise. He knows all and see all. I still trust in Jesus because there's power in that name, there's peace in that name, there's joy in that name, there's salvation in that name, and there is no other name given among men. The word of God says in, *Isaiah 43:2 says when you pass through the waters, I will be with you; and when you pass through the rivers, they will not sweep over you. When you walk through the fire, you will not be burned; the flames will not set you ablaze.* No matter what I was going through, I knew God was with me. I stood up, dried my tears, went to my bedroom, opened my closet to pick out my best suit, fixed my hair and makeup, got dressed, and went to the house of the Lord.

Chapter Sixteen

Here We Go ...

At the church, we had a full house. I entered from the pastor's study like a first lady and sat down in the minister's wives session. Something seemed to be a little off. But I didn't care; I was covered by the blood of Jesus. I looked around, and it seemed like all fifteen hundred members were in the house. I looked, over to my left, and even Sister Bunny was in her Sunday best. If only the members knew about the leadership of this church. Bruce and his mother could preach the roof off the house, but they were so lost. The other ministers of the church were genuine but, clueless because Bruce's mother was the bookkeeper of the church. Oh, no! There are blue uniforms everywhere. The police just walked into the church and serve a warrant for Bruce's mother's arrest. I tell people all the time be careful how you treat people you could be in their place next. What you reap, you will sow. Bruce's mother started resisting arrest, so they threw her to the ground and cuffed her. The police cuffed Bruce and then they cuffed me. I couldn't believe it. I was being placed under arrest. So we all were howl off to jail. I was placed in holding and I was questioned by five different officers about the operation of the church. I couldn't tell them anything because I knew nothing. They always kept me in the dark. I was nervous and crying. They held me for six hours and released me. I'm many things, but, I'm no snitch. As I walked out of the cell into the lobby area, I saw my mother waiting, I ran to her and cried in her arms like an infant. She told me it was going to be alright. I asked her how she know where I was, and she told me motor mouth Rita was there when I was arrested. Lord sure do work in mysterious ways. I was never so happy to see my mother. I looked up, and there where the prayer warrior from my home church and my pastor. God is so good. If he doesn't do anything else, he has still done more than enough.

Chapter Seventeen

My Test Begins...

Two months had passed since I took the HIV test. I finally dared to open my test results. It was negative, but I was to be tested every six months. I was so relieved. I blessed God for His Grace and Mercy. Then I began to think about Bruce. Hadn't seen or heard from him, but he was still my husband, and I felt that since he didn't call me I needed to go and check on him. Motor mouth, Rita. Had kept me informed about everything that was going on at the church. She told me they found Craig dead in an alley. It appears he was murdered. Bruce's mother was sentenced to 10 years, and he was released with 15 years' probation because he was willing to testify against his mother. I decided to go over there, but my mother was against it. I had to make her understand he was still my husband. She finally agreed. I went to my former home to find Bruce lying in the middle of the floor, sick. He had thrown up everywhere. He looked at me and said go ahead and laugh. I know you're happy to see me on my ass. I told him I was there because I was concerned. He told me to get my things out of his house and said he would give me a divorce. I helped him up from the floor and sat him up on the sofa. It looked like he had lost about 20 pounds. I asked him was he hungry; he said no. He just wanted me to get out. I got angry with him and went to the bedroom but then turned around and went back into the living room and told him I was going to help him whether he wanted me to or not. I saw a medical paper on the table and I read it. He had HIV. He looked at me and said now you know. He asked me did if I had it and I told him no. He said good because you don't deserve it. I just looked at him. I wanted to say. Oh, I guess I deserved gonorrhea and syphilis that he gave me. Okay, Lord Hold my tongue, I didn't come over here for this. Anyway, he said that the doctor gave him six months. I ask him if he knew who gave it to him. He said Craig, rest his soul. I asked him why, he said that. He admitted that he killed Craig. I asked him why he was telling me all this. He said because he was going to die anyway. I thought he was telling me that because he was going to do something to me. But anyway. I had to ask him why? Why did he marry me, and he knew he was bisexual. He just looked at me, and finally, out of desperation, he told me about his enduring sexual lure for men. I thanked him for his honesty. He asked me to forgive him, and I did. I did it for me because I didn't want to be attached to what he did to me. I know I have to work through my forgiveness for me to be totally healed. Because I was still very angry with Bruce. I had to find a way to disconnect from him healthily. I knew only God could give me the strength to endure the season that I was in. So, I helped him get cleaned up and I gave him something to eat and his meds, but he refused to take the meds. I left them on the table. He told me he needed to get some rest I helped him to bed and he fell fast asleep. I sat on the side of the bed and thought about how happy we used to be. I couldn't believe it came to this. Truly, I couldn't leave him like this. So I went home to my mother's house to get a few things and told her I had to go home, I had to take care of my husband. I didn't want to, but God had, mercy on me and forgiven me. I had to do the same for Bruce.

Day by day, it seemed like Bruce was losing his battle; he had grown so angry with God. He was so weak. I finally got tired of him trying to kill himself. I grabbed my Bible, and I walked through the house, praying and blessing every room. I even prayed over Bruce. He refused the blessing; he told me to stop. I just kept praying, and finally, with a scream, he said God, I'm sorry. He repented before God. He started crying and telling God everything he was sorry for. I kneeled at his side and prayed some more. I was blessing God for what he was doing at that moment. No words could explain what was going on. Funny how life can be calm one moment and trouble the next. But God was watching and working the whole thing out. Once we finish praying, I fixed him something to eat, helped him with his bath, and got him to bed. As I was cleaning, I saw that there were many bills passed due and a lot of hate mail. It's funny how people say that they love you, but the minute you make a mistake, they hate you. Lord, have mercy. I started thinking about my mother and I wasn't sure if I wanted to go through any more drama with her. I didn't think I was strong enough. All I knew was that God would be with me. How did I know this? Because God has always found me in times of trouble. Trouble doesn't come by itself; it comes in a pack. But I know God will take care of me no matter what.

Sure thing…
God is able, but you must fight to get back to him, especially when you have been let down

Chapter Nineteen

Sunday Morning...

Early on Sunday morning, I got up and started getting ready for church. Bruce knocked on my door and asked if he could go to church with me. I said yes. I helped him get dressed, and he started crying. He asked me why I was doing all the things I was doing. I said, because I loved him. He asked me how I could love a man who caused me so much pain. I said, because of God mercy and grace. He looked at me and told me he was sorry. I said I had already forgiven him. He continued to cry, and I told him to dry his tears because God is able and he should not feel sorry for himself. I felt at that moment that if I ever loved Bruce, it was my responsibility to get him to Jesus. As I help him change his depend, I couldn't look him in the face; I wanted him to keep the little dignity he had left. As we finished we headed out and arrived on time at the church; not just any church service, but my home church, Holy Ghost filled. Bruce and I walked in side by side the stares we got what was so lukewarm. It didn't matter because I came to hear a word from the Lord. My mother was there and looked upon me with disappointment in her eyes. She was embarrassed. I saw Sister Lewis leaning over to whisper something in her ear. My mother dropped her head and then waved for us to come sit with her. Bruce was so weak, but I had enough strength for the both of us. Don't get me wrong; I was not in love with Bruce anymore but I loved him and I wanted to be by his side to witness him give himself totally to Jesus. You know, only God can transform us. I was sitting here with a man who was broken. But that is when God can really do something with you. When you sin. First you hate it. Then you love it. Then you come to depend upon it. But God has to tear it down to take out what he has put in you. I know because he broke me and put me back together. God can use your brokenness because we are his children and he loves us. As written in Roman 10:9 that if you confess with your mouth the Lord Jesus and believe in your heart that God has raised Him from the dead, you will be saved.

Chapter Twenty
Sister Visit ...

We, just arrived from church. I helped him out his clothes and put him to bed, then got started on dinner. Just as I entered the living room, the devil met me. He said here is a young woman taking care of a man who has beaten, rape, and misused her, and she is here changing his diaper. Are you crazy? I froze instantly in place as I began to think and second guess myself why? Although my mind was playing tricks on me, in my heart, I felt it was the right thing to do. I said out loud satan I rebuke you in the name of Jesus! Then the doorbell rang.

It was the sisters from the church. I was so surprised. They had food and everything and they told me they had come to help me, and Bruce. I was so overwhelmed, especially when I saw my mother. I hugged her in the middle of my living room, and the sisters begun to sing. I was able to let go of some things and I bless God at the top of my lungs for all he had done and all he was doing. All night, all day, God kept angel watching over me.

Chapter Twenty One

Final Stage ...

After two months, Bruce took a turn for the worse. Everyone was there, including his biological mother Bernice. Bernice and Bruce had rebuilt their relationship, and she has been a big beacon of hope for me. My mother and the other sisters were there for me. We prepared a schedule for each of us to take turns to sit with Bruce. Even Sister Mattie he cussed and threw out the house. Thank God for them all because they sat with Bruce and read the word of God to him and prayed with him as he began to make his transition from this old world. I stood in the doorway watching Sister Mattie praying and singing amazing grace to Bruce as he lay flat on his back gasping for air. I knew it wouldn't be long now. All the family Bruce had was in that room. There was no one else. By the time Sister Mattie finished her song, Bruce had looked over at me like he was telling me goodbye and then looked up to the ceiling, and he closed his eyes, and then he was gone. I closed my eyes and said a prayer. I called for the other Sisters. I went to call the coroner, and the Sisters began praying and singing. As I return back to the bedroom, I smiled and kissed the face of the man I once loved. As he went into his long sleep, I looked up to God and said thank you, not because I was finally free, but because I passed the test. How many of you know there's no testimony without a test. There was no way I could have walked out on Bruce; my blessing was tied up in him. There was no way I was going to let him keep it. What God has joined together, let no man separate. The truth is, I don't believe God put us together. I picked him, but I stood before God and said I do. And I stayed to help my husband because he couldn't help himself. And I know in my heart, that God will forever bless me. I know some may ask, why did I stay? I stayed because, to get Bruce to Jesus, he had to first see him through me. I didn't need to remind Bruce of what he did to me because my presents and my kindness remind him every day I was there. In this life, there will come a time, you have to make tough decisions, and when that time comes remember to operate out of faith and not fear. It's really not what happens to you but how you handle it. Every tear I have cried, everything I been through will not be wasted. This Christian life is not a 100-yard dash, it's a marathon. You don't run until you get tired; you run until you die. From birth to death, life is a struggle.

"For God has not given us the spirit of fear; but of power, and of love, and of a sound mind." Believe that, and you too will survive.

THE
POETRY CORNER

Sometimes, when you ride through a storm, you look for an answer, you look for help, you look for protection, and you can't find it. You look to friends and family, and still you get nothing. Some people doubt what you're saying, but you know you are going through a storm—you know you are under extreme pressure. No one seems to understand what you are going through. And they probably never will, just thank God that you are alive. You see, I'm an old woman, and I have been through some things. I was 13 years old when I became a mother. Back in the old days, you would have been considered an adult ready for whatever came your way. I didn't have much schooling because my mama told me that wasn't important. She said what was important was washing, ironing, cooking, and cleaning so you could keep a man. I knew there was more to life than lying on my back.

I was a queen; I had many dreams. I wanted to do big things. But the babies kept coming. By the time I was 20 I had six kids, and I was their mother and father. It was my storm that I created because I didn't consult the Father about the man who gave me three sons and three daughters my life was out of order. My kids became grown, and I grew older, and once again I became my grandkids' mother. What my mother taught me I taught to my kids, and the family curse started all over again. My kids became mothers and fathers—even my 13-year-old granddaughter has a baby daughter. I was too old to start over again. I tried to win my oldest daughter from her best friend. That crack did her in; when she died, I was left to be a mother once again. We are family. That's what they said, but when times got hard, all the other sisters and brothers walked away, even though I gave birth to them all the same way. How could they leave their mother out to dry, standing alone with tears in her eyes? How could they leave a woman who gave all she had? I got blisters and bags trying to give them what I never had. My sons married women of another color and forgot that their skin is the same color as their mother's. I had grandkids in and out of jail, taking my social security check, using it to make bail. Y'all, let me tell you, I been through the storms, I been through hell. But I survived the storm because God never left my side—He caught the tears that fell from my eyes. But when I think about storms, I think about Job. Satan was mad at God because God had a man who would stand for him and not compromise. He created storm after storm for Job. He killed his children. He took his wealth, took his health, but he couldn't take his faith. In this life, storms will come, but learn to live in your storms until God gives you the victory. When you can't go any further, when you can't take any more, when you feel like you're breaking, when you feel like you're falling apart, when you feel like you can't get a prayer through, when you feel like everybody is against you, and nothing is working anymore, just remember, God's grace is sufficient. satan wants to break you, but remember, God will keep you.

I'm a full-figured black woman loving and embracing every curve on my body I'm bold, and sometimes I can be a little cold. Never could be bought with gold

I'm my mother's child, who used to run a little wild looking for everything I thought I wanted. Looking for a dream that I never seen looking for a man, when he only wanted to get in my pants looking for someone to love me when I didn't know how to love myself. Looking for me that I couldn't see I lived in a place called yesterday I lived in a place that was darker than night. I crossed many roads that were cold as ice. I cried myself to sleep many nights because it was dark and I could not see where to go. Until one day someone came with the key I started to scream out, please set me free. It was my Father who opened the door. I'd never seen a light so bright Oh, I can see the day for the future I can see my hope for tomorrow. I can feel my Father present, yes, he is the only

one who was able to deliver me now can you
see, can you really see. That's why I'm loving
me, I'm loving me, I'm loving me.

 God is the man who created your heart and soul
the one who can deliver you from all strongholds
He knows when you fall back into yourself, giving
some to him and some you kept.

Like a man who's in your blood,
The one who takes your mind,
Plays with it and releases it, time after time,
getting in line, waiting for the next time. And you
ask yourself why, why do you go back, when you
know he's not all that, not even some, except
when he's using his tongue that's been on other
buns?

You ask yourself why, why can't I put him out of
my mind? Closing the door, but I keep letting him
come in and hurt me more.

Is it because I don't want to be alone?
Is it because I have kids? Is it because I have low
self-esteem?

All may be true, but when will I draw the line and
say that I'm through?

Well I guess I just love that man, and I don't care what anyone says, but is he worth me not walking through the pearly gates?

Pimping

I'm tired of all the lies, men getting between my thighs, and when I see them with other women, they want to lie. Why do I get played? Used and abused, my heart feeling so untrue to myself because all I know to be is someone else. Living off empty promises and broken dreams, broke pocketbook, doing crooked things, sometimes thinking I'm insane. Living off welfare, thinking like a queen, waiting for different men to buy me things, but no, not one, ever buys the damn wedding ring. I'm tired of rocking the sheets. The gates are closed. It's time for me to start living like a lady and stop pimping myself as a hoe. When I saw myself outside of the frame, I was reminded that it's all in the Name. In the Name! Protect the Name!

Let me tell you something: no matter what goes on in your life, GOD is there. If you feel your life is at a point of no return ask yourself, how do you survive the storm when your world is turned upside down? When your world is dark and when your mind has been taken hostage? How do you survive a storm when you have given all you have and left nothing for yourself, and no one seems to care. How do you survive the storm when your health has failed, when you can't take care of yourself and you feel like you want to trade life for death. How do you survive the storm when your marriage has failed? When you find out that you were really sleeping with the enemy. How do you survive the storm when people have lied to you, tricked you, manipulated you, and abused you, broadcasting your business on every TV channel. How do you survive the storm, when you have spent your whole life trying to live up to other people's notion of you? When you dealt with people telling you, you are nothing, you are never going to be nothing, because you a slut like your mama and a whoremonger like your daddy, a hypocrite like your granny, and drunk like your granddaddy. I'm talking about a generational curse. How do you survive the storm? How do you survive the storm after just getting saved and welcomed into God's family as a little babe. I think to myself, did I make a mistake coming this way, when my brother and sister in Christ are supposed to love me and they hurt me anyway. I stop looking at man and I start looking at God, and I say, Lord, I know you love me because you the one who saved me and touched my heart. How do you survive the storm? Well, I got good news. Storms do pass. No matter what kind of storm it is, it has to pass. Every now and then, a storm needs to come to blow some people, stuff, and things, out of your life. I no longer worry about what people say about me, and I know longer worry about what that they think about me. Why? Because they were not there when I was fighting for my mind. When my enemies were telling me I wasn't worth a dime. They weren't there, when the grace of God found me in my darkness, in my addiction, in my situation, in my dependencies, in my guilt, and in my past. I confess that I needed a savior, and when he rescued me, I chose life over death instantly. When I think about my storms, I think about Matthew 8:23-27 -And when he got into the boat, his disciples followed him. And, behold, there arose a great storm on the sea, so that the boat was being swamped by the waves; but he was asleep. And they went and woke him, saying, "Save us, Lord; we are perishing." And he said to them, "Why are you afraid, O you of little faith?" Then he rose and rebuked the winds and the sea, and there was a great calm. And the men marveled, saying, "What sort of man is this, that even winds and sea obey him? "It's good to know that God can speak to your storm. Sometimes storms in our life test our faith, so when the storm comes, anchor yourself down in the Lord and ride the storm out with confidence in Him. And if you trust God and not afraid, and if you recognize that you're not alone, you will survive your storm. My dear friend, you can make it!

- Sometime the true is in the joke. He showed me himself, but I didn't believe him. I looked the other way.

- Never dismiss bad behavior: I let him disrespect me as a woman. I went along with it because I was intrigued by him.

- Stand for what you believe in: I compromised my self-worth for only half of a man.

- Don't change who you are to please others: God made you. And what he made is already perfect.

- Remember God and your family is all you got at the beginning, in the middle, and at the end. Don't turn on God and your family. Sometimes love makes you do crazy things. Thank God he is an unchanging God.

The enemy wants you to accept your situation as a new standard; remember, the devil never has the last word concerning your story. God is the Beginning and the End!

Annie Johnson

Amazon Prime

Stage Plays

www.awjproduction.com